The Boy Who Cried ALiEN

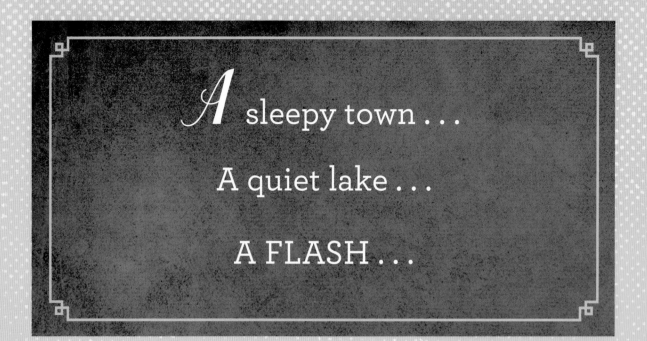

A sleepy town . . .

A quiet lake . . .

A FLASH . . .

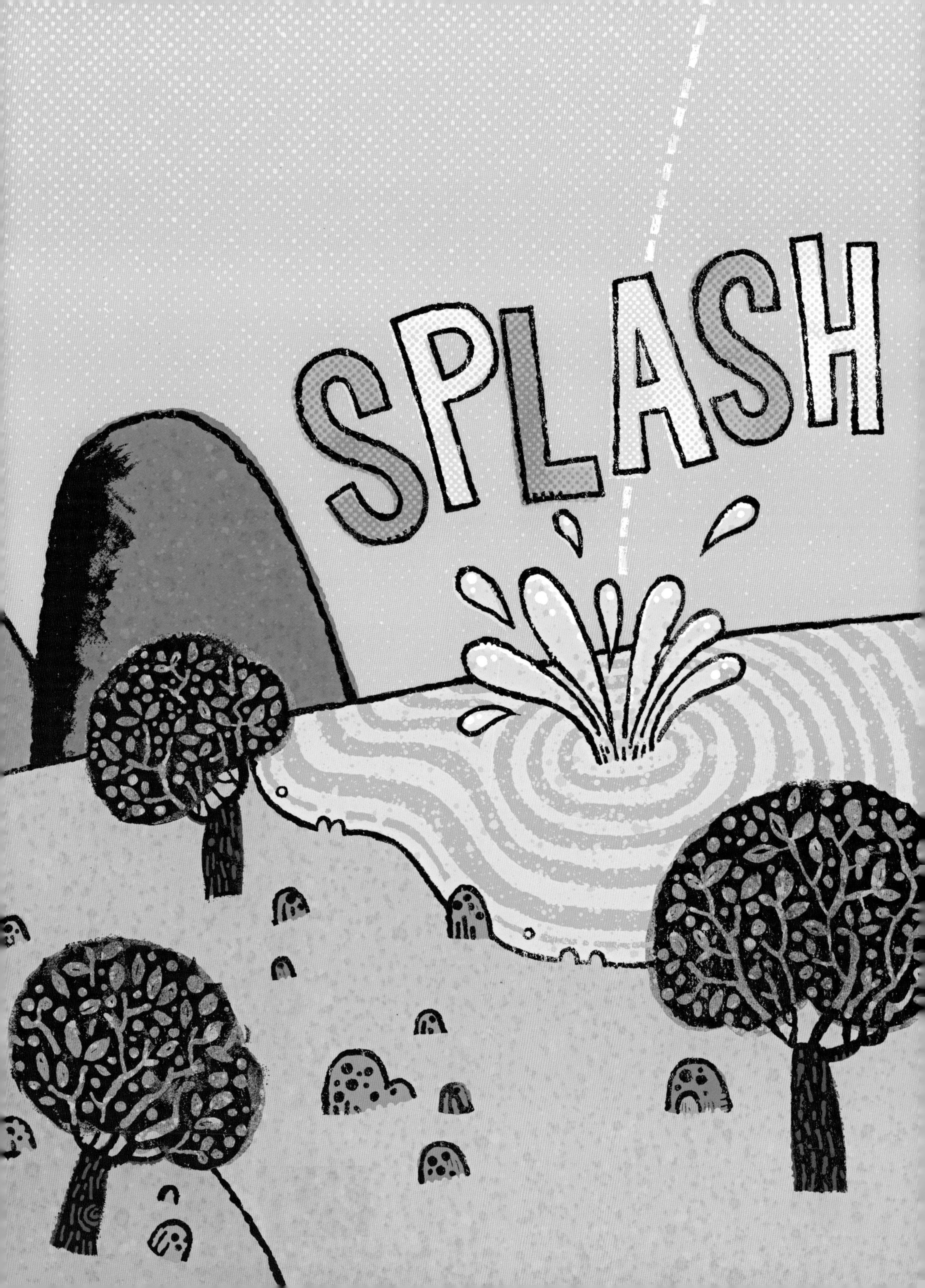
SPLASH

To Max and Kara
—M.S.

For Sacha,
Wilson,
and Elliot
—B.B.

Thanks to Steve Aronson, Donna Bray, Tamson Weston, and to Rotem Moscovich and all the other good folks at Disney • Hyperion. —M.S.

First Edition
10 9 8 7 6 5 4 3 2 1
F850-6835-5-11349
Printed in China • Reinforced binding
This book is set in Archer, Century, and BaseMono.
The art was created with India ink on Bristol board, scanned, and completed with digital color-juice.
Book design by Whitney Manger

Library of Congress Cataloging-in-Publication Data
Singer, Marilyn.
   The boy who cried alien / written by Marilyn Singer; illustrated by Brian Biggs.—1st ed.
       p. cm.
   Summary: A boy known for telling lies announces that aliens have landed in Malarkey Lake, and not surprisingly, no one believes him.
   ISBN 978-0-7868-3825-7
   [1. Stories in rhyme. 2. Extraterrestrial beings—Fiction. 3. Honesty—Fiction. 4. Humorous stories.] I. Biggs, Brian, ill. II. Title.
   PZ8.3.S6154Boy 2012
   [E]—dc22   2011008459

Visit www.disneyhyperionbooks.com

The Boy Who Cried ALIEN

words by MARILYN SINGER   pictures by BRIAN BIGGS

Disney • Hyperion Books • New York

I told my friends that Dad's a secret agent guy
out searching for the lost world of Atlantis.
That Mom was bitten by a bat and thinks she'll fly.
Her favorite foods are moth and praying mantis.

I told my class that Bigfoot's prowling 'round the school.
He really likes to shower in the gym.
The reason why he won't bathe in the swimming pool
is 'cause a whale arrived ahead of him.

And now a spaceship's landed in Malarkey Lake.
It looks just like a giant gold-capped tooth.
It's over there and I can swear it's not a fake.
What could I say that's stranger than the truth?

My dear prevaricating pal,
oh, the tales that you created,
    the events that you inflated!
Yes, your fibs were highly rated.
But, come on—*aliens from space?*
How corny, quaint, and uninspired.
I can't be fooled by stuff that tired.
Better whoppers are required
    or, my flimflam friend, you're fired!

I saw them landing.
I saw them standing
on pale blue legs right over here. . . .

A scary pair
with crazy hair.
How could they up and disappear?

And where's their ship?
I'm gonna flip!
That massive molar simply vanished?

Hey, wait . . . come back!
Look, here's a track. . . .

Carlig and Dreab investigate the town.
Aliens, aliens!
Are they here to raid us, invade us?
Will they probe my frontal lobe?
GROCERY
21
MEAT

Klatu, nanoo, how-do-you-do!
In peace you surely come.
Would you mind informing me
    what galaxy you're from?
I'd love to see your spaceship.
Perhaps you'd let me man it.
I've never even left my town—
    please take me to your planet!

Mother taught me guests are guests,

   be they from Italy, Chile, Missouri,

   Canada, Kenya, or Alpha Centauri.

Offer refreshments, be conversational

   (avoid any topic that's much too sensational):

"The weather is lovely. . . . There might be a storm. . . .

   I admire your sweater/shirt/skirt/uniform. . . .

Um, you say that's your *skin*? Oh my and oh me.

Do have another biscuit and a second cup of tea."

Please don't hurt me, don't get rough.

(You can call me names, but that's enough!)

Don't abduct me, or put me in storage.

Don't deconstruct me, or turn me to porridge.

I kind of don't mind providing you merriment—

    as long as I'm not someone's science experiment.

I may appear strong, but I'm not really tough.

I don't fight, I don't bite—I just make up weird stuff.

I do it for fun, and allow me to mention,

    it makes me feel special; it gets me attention.

But after today I might give up my act.

Fiction is suddenly duller than fact.

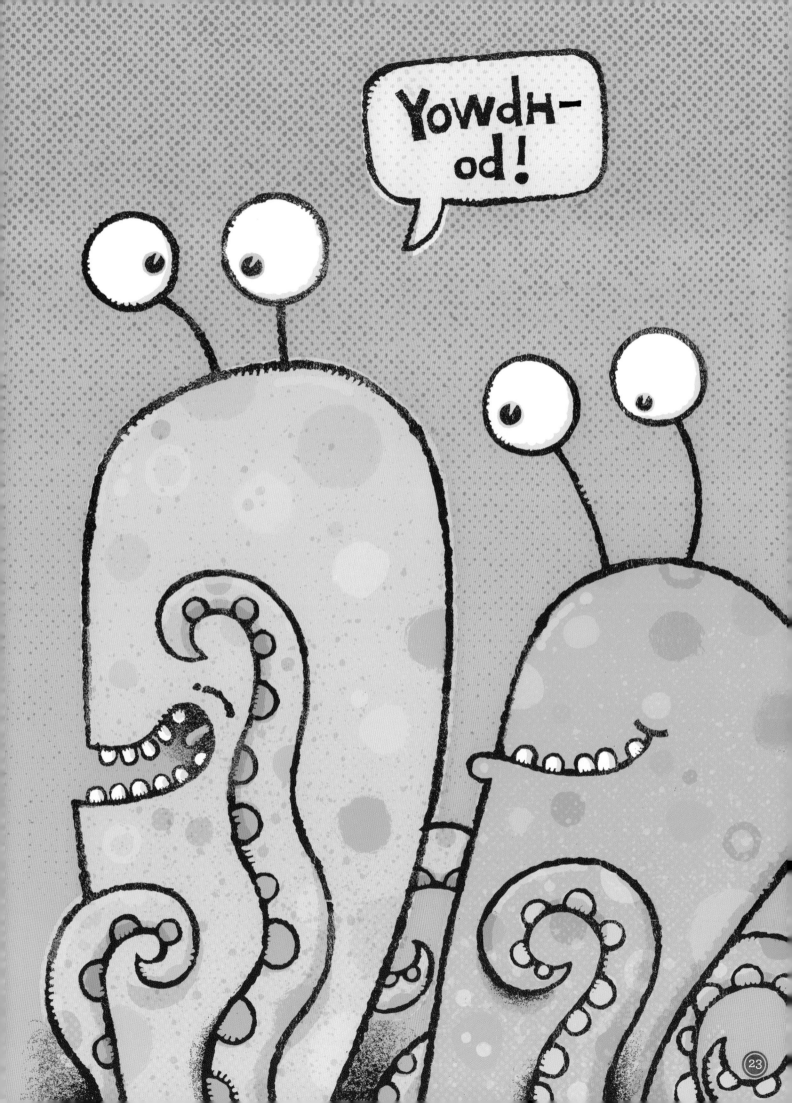

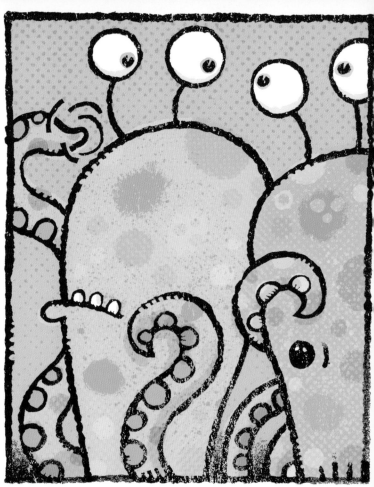

The aliens put the Rranslatot—the Translator—on Larry's head.

You're off to Hollywood? Ha! That lie is pretty good!

Yes. Martians are bad at lying.
So are vegans. But on our planet . . .
good lying's an art; how it can amaze!
It's worthy of cheers and many bouquets.

26

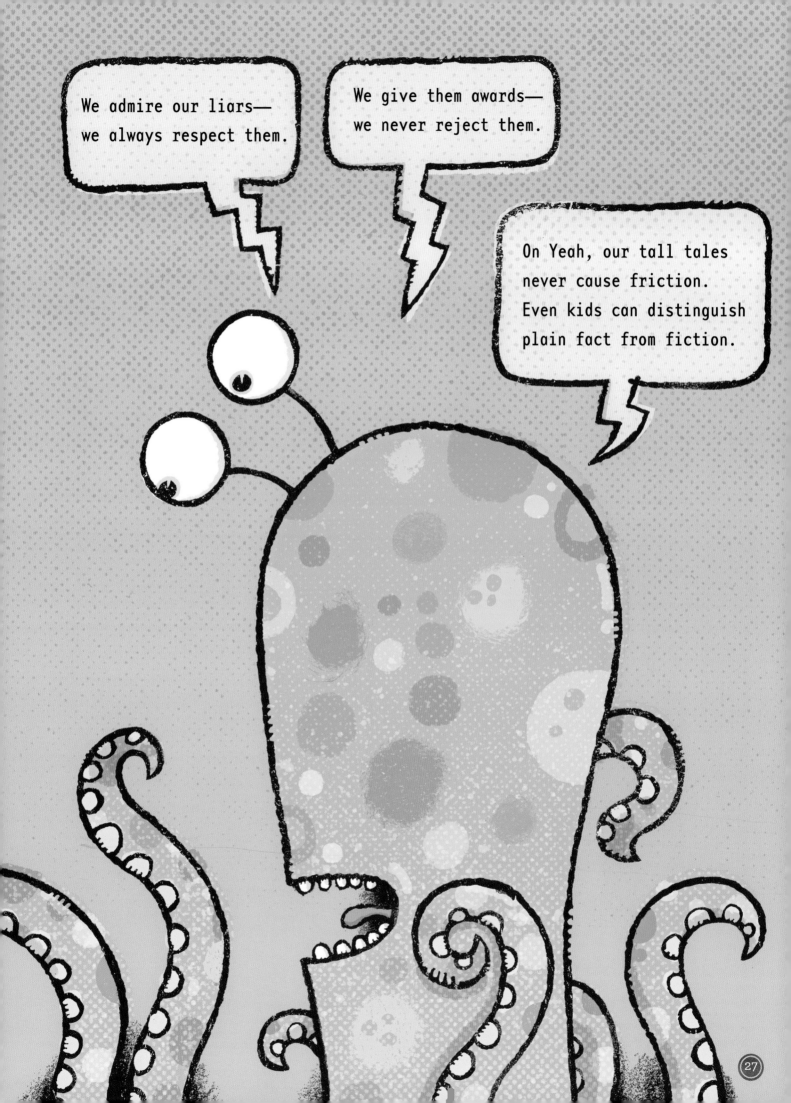

Just a few perfect burps
and we won't have to roam.
We will be on our way
to the zons up at home.

Quick, grab that zon!

Zon burp fuel? I know that zon!
Her name is Bessie. She's a Holstein,
   and my closest pal.
These visitors are friendly, Bessie.
So don't be frightened, gal!

There you are! Don't keep your distance.
Our alien pals need your assistance.
   See this tube? Please don't squelch
   your natural bovine urge to belch.

Larry gets a statue in his honor—and the chance to open the Yeah School of Fabulous Fibbing in his own hometown.

LARRY

A Note on Translation

To read the alien language, reverse the first and last letters of a word: e.g. *yorthw* is "worthy." However, if the word is a plural, the "s" still stays at the end: *rials* is "liars." If the word is the past tense of a verb, the "ed" also stays at the end: e.g. *lulped* is "pulled" (though *dleasep* is "pleased"). A few words don't translate at all: *zon* (kind of like a cow); and *Yeah* (the planet's name).

You'll notice that the poems in the alien language are not translated word for word. When translators translate poetry from another language, they work hard to make it sound poetic. Here is one word-for-word example to help you figure out the code. The poetic translations for the rest of the alien language poems are on the next page.

Word-for-word translation of page 7

Kaput rocket, no more gas.
Oy vey! Shoot me now.
When he looks in the garage,
Pop will have a zon.

Translations

Page 7

Busted thrusters, out of power.
Yikes! We've done it now.
When he sees we took the ship,
    Dad will have a cow.

Pages 10–11

We can't hang out here on the grass.
We need a zon to give us gas.
Where's one to send us back to space?
Come on, let's explore this place.

We'll keep our eyes open
    and watch out for surprises.
You veil the ship.
I'll get our disguises.

Pages 20–21

It has four legs, not six.
It has no proud red comb.
But still it resembles
    the zons up at home.

It eats grasses, not rocks,
    and its horns aren't chrome.
But it moos and it chews like
    the zons up at home.

Oh, zon, we've been foolish
    and very uncool.
So we're begging you, please,
    can you spare us some fuel?

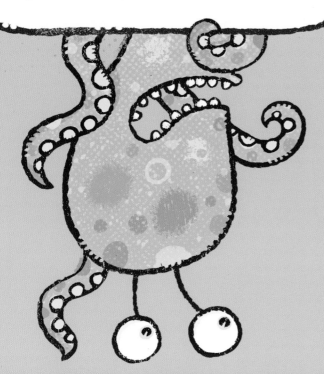